Nickerbacher

Terry John Barto

Nickerbacher

Printed in the United States of America

Illustrations by Kim Sponaugle

Paperback ISBN: 978-1-944878-27-6

Contents

Chapter One
The Dream
1

Chapter Two
The Prince
9

Chapter Three
The City
21

Chapter Four
The Audition
29

Chapter Five
The Coach
37

Chapter Six
The Show
45

Chapter One
The Dream

Once upon a time, a starry-eyed dragon named Nickerbacher stood guard for Princess Gwendolyn in a tall, tall tower in the valley north of La La Land.

Nickerbacher and Gwendolyn became friends. Every evening, they watched *The Late Knight Show*, a television program featuring a variety of live performances. Just before the end of the hour, host Johnny Kingston said, "Want to be on *The Late Knight Show*? You can! Go to our website to find out how to audition!"

"That's my dream!" Nickerbacher declared. "I want to go to La La Land and be a comedian on *The Late Knight Show*!"

"You have to get better jokes, then," Princess Gwendolyn said.

"I have great jokes!" Nickerbacher jumped in front of the TV. "Why did I take forever to cross the road?"

"I don't know," she said.

"Because I'm always a-draggin'."

Nickerbacher rolled on the floor, laughing.

Princess Gwendolyn rolled her eyes. "Nice try…but no."

"No?! Why not?" Nickerbacher said.

"Comedy requires more than puns," the princess said. "With some practice, I think you'd make a great comedian."

Nickerbacher shivered. "Don't let my papa hear that. You know what he always says..."

"Every dragon has a duty to guard princesses!" they quoted together.

"But it's more than that," Nickerbacher said. "We're not allowed to do anything else. We don't have the same rights as humans. They think we're dangerous."

Princess Gwendolyn put her hand on Nickerbacher's snout. "Which is why you need to tell your story. Be yourself and people will love you like I do."

"You're right," Nickerbacher said. "I'll tell Papa. Again."

Princess Gwendolyn smiled. "That's my dragon."

Just then, the floor started to shake. "It's him!" Nickerbacher whispered.

A gust of wind blew with great force. Trees fell over. Animals scurried away. Nickerbacher flew into his guard position just in time.

"Good evening, son," Papa Dragon said. "Fight any princes today?"

Nickerbacher hesitated.

Papa frowned. "Well?"

The princess elbowed Nickerbacher. He blurted, "I think humans and dragons can live together in harmony, Papa!"

"Whaaaaat?!?" Papa roared.

Shaking, Nickerbacher stepped up on a tree stump. "What do you get when you cross a dragon with a snowman?"

Papa just stared.

"A puddle," Nickerbacher answered.

Papa breathed fire. "What are you talking about?"

"I want a chance to prove to the world that dragons aren't dangerous."

Nickerbacher swallowed. "I want to be a stand-up comedian!"

"Again with the comedy thing. We're dragons," Papa hollered. "We guard princesses! My father guarded princesses, his father guarded princesses!"

"But I want to make people laugh!" Nickerbacher wailed.

"You're a dragon. You're not supposed to make people laugh," Papa growled.

Nickerbacher sniffed. "But Johnny Kingston said *anybody* can audition for *The Late Knight Show*."

"Son, it's important to understand that not everybody is like you," Papa Dragon said. "If you give humans a chance, they'll hurt you. That's what humans do."

Gwendolyn put her hands on her hips. "Excuse me?"

He glared at the princess. "*Princes* are human and look at how *they* treat dragons."

Nickerbacher hung his head. "Okay, Papa."

Papa Dragon took flight. "I promise, Nickerbacher, this is for your own good."

"He'll come around," Princess Gwendolyn said. "Now, let's get to work."

Nickerbacher looked up. "Yeah, but..."

"You need better material," Princess Gwendolyn said. "Great comedy always has two secret ingredients."

"Like chocolate and marshmallows?" Nickerbacher asked.

Princess Gwendolyn chuckled. "Close, but more like truth and heart."

CHAPTER TWO
THE PRINCE

The next day, a prince arrived to rescue Princess Gwendolyn, who sat under a tree in her pajamas, reading aloud from a book. Nickerbacher was half asleep in the branches, listening to the princess. "And the prince leaned down and gave Sleeping Beauty a kiss," Gwendolyn read.

The princess and Nickerbacher looked at each other, confused. "Why would he kiss someone who's sleeping?" Nickerbacher asked.

"I have no idea. These fairy tales make no sense to me," Gwendolyn replied.

The prince cleared his throat. He shuffled through note cards.

"Not again." Nickerbacher pulled his head back into the branches. "This is the fifth prince this week!" he mumbled.

Princess Gwendolyn snapped the book shut. "What is this, your first day?"

"Y-y-yes!" the prince stammered. "I mean, no."

He held up a note card. "Um, the Prince Guild has sent me to rescue Princess Gwendolyn…I'm here to rescue …" He turned the card over. "…you."

Princess Gwendolyn gestured to herself. "In my pajamas?"

"I don't care what you look like," the prince said. "The Guild ordered me to rescue you, so you're being rescued." He reached toward her.

"Back off, pal, or you're gonna have to deal with something scarier than an angry princess," she said.

The prince lowered his hand. "If it's your sense in fashion, I've already survived that."

"Here's a hint," Princess Gwendolyn said. "It starts with a D and ends with Ragon."

"Let's see. I assume Ragon is Italian in origin. Is it pasta?" the prince said.

Nickerbacher slid down from the tree. "No, but my grandfather was Italian."

The prince turned to face Nickerbacher. "Uh - uh – dragon!"

Princess Gwendolyn sighed. "What did you expect? Everyone knows dragons guard princesses!"

The prince referred to another note card. "I'm P-p-p-prince Hap-ha-ha-ha-"

"Prince Hap Haha," Nickerbacher said.

"N-n-n-no," the prince stuttered.

"Prince Happy?" Gwendolyn put in.

"Prince NOT Happy?" Nickerbacher asked.

"Prince Happening?" Gwendolyn added.

"No!" the prince shouted. "Prince Happenstance!"

Nickerbacher grinned. "Prince Fancypants?"

The prince threw down the note cards. "This is not how it's supposed to go! If I don't bring back the princess, I'll be kicked out of the Prince Guild!"

Nickerbacher used his tail to swipe Prince Happenstance off his feet. He snorted. "That reminds me of a joke. What do you get when - "

The prince scrambled to his feet. "D-d-don't kill me, dragon. Please."

"I'm a comedian," Nickerbacher said. "I'll slay you with laughter, Fancypants!"

The prince attempted a regal pose. "My name is ***Happenstance***! Now step aside, dragon. I really need to rescue this princess."

Nickerbacher shook his head. "Don't you think I'm funny?"

"No offense, but name calling isn't very funny," the prince said. He quickly drew out his sword, but it flew from his hand and into the side of a tree.

Princess Gwendolyn waved to get their attention. "Hello!"

The prince darted to the tree, pulled his sword from the trunk and fell on his behind. “Ow!”

Princess Gwendolyn gave a sharp whistle. “If anybody cares, I don’t want to be rescued!”

Prince Happenstance plugged his ears. “And I’m ignoring what you just said.”

“Tell the Prince Guild I’m staying here in protest,” the princess said. “It’s not fair that dragons are second-class citizens. They should have the same rights as everyone else!”

“Don’t be foolish, Highness. Dragons are *third*-class citizens,” Prince Happenstance said. “Now, dragon, are you gonna fight me?”

Nickerbacher yawned. “If you insist. How about some fire?” He flew to the top of the tower and breathed a scorching stream into the sky.

Prince Happenstance lowered his sword. “Um, weren’t you supposed to shoot that flame at me?”

“Like this?” Nickerbacher said. He jumped off the tower and dive-bombed the prince, who hit the ground. Nickerbacher landed with a thud, lifted his head and belched. A puff of smoke bellowed out.

Using the smoke as a cover, the prince grabbed Princess Gwendolyn and tossed her toward his horse and missed. She sailed over the saddle and tumbled into a flower-covered bush. “Oops,” he said, and reached down to help her up.

Gwendolyn grabbed him by his neck. “ARE YOU OUT OF YOUR MIND!?”

“What?” the prince choked.

Princess Gwendolyn let go of him. “You threw me into a bush!”

The prince gasped for air. “But it’s honeysuckle. Flowers are soft, and don’t they smell good?”

Prince Happenstance offered his hand again. Princess Gwendolyn slapped it away.

Nickerbacher swooped in between them. “Want me to roast him, princess? It’s not my usual thing, but I’ll do it for you.”

The prince’s jaw dropped. “You’re joking, right?”

Nickerbacher took a step forward. “Rawrrr.”

“Help!” the prince squeaked.

“Wait! I have an idea,” Princess Gwendolyn said. She leaned over to Nickerbacher. “We’re going to let him rescue me.”

Nickerbacher scratched his head. "Why?"

"Yeah, why?" the prince asked.

"If the prince succeeds, you must chase after me, right?" She winked. "What if we ended up in La La Land?"

"I'd have to follow you, I guess," Nickerbacher said.

"Exactly!" Princess Gwendolyn nodded. "And if you follow us all the way to La La Land, you could maybe look for us at, say, *The Late Knight Show*."

Nickerbacher jumped up and down. "I could audition for Johnny Kingston!" He stopped. "But you don't like what La La Land stands for. That's why you chose to stay here."

"This is our chance to do something about it!" the princess exclaimed. "We could make a difference."

Prince Happenstance raised his hand. "Don't I have a say in this?"

"Sorry," the princess said. "It's important to Nickerbacher and he's my friend."

Prince Happenstance frowned. "A dragon and a princess? Friends?"

"Yes!" the princess cried.

"Ugh...." The prince dropped on the ground. "I'm out of the Guild for sure."

"Stop whining! This is a worthier cause than the lousy Prince Guild," Gwendolyn said. "Don't you want to do something more important than kill a dragon?"

"I'm thinking," Prince Happenstance said.

"BE a prince! Help us!" the princess exclaimed.

The prince straightened up. "Fine. I'll do it."

"We're a team!" Nickerbacher said. "But what about my act?"

Princess Gwendolyn hugged him. "We'll help you along the way. Right, Happenstance? Now, let me get out of these PJs."

CHAPTER THREE
THE CITY

The princess locked up the tower and the trio fled the valley. As they traveled, Nickerbacher tried one joke after another on the prince and princess.

"What about your home?" Happenstance said. "Families can be really funny sometimes."

"My mom is pretty funny, actually," Nickerbacher said.

"Too bad you don't know my family," Happenstance said. "They're the stuff jokes are made of..."

"That's it," the princess said. "Tell jokes about your family."

GRIFFIN PARK 2
LA LA LAND
LA LA LAND
fairywood
FOREVER
CEMETARY
LAX
MEDIEVAL
TAR
PITS

LALA LAND
OPEN
DELI
HOTEL
HOTEL

They took the scenic route through Griffin Park and into La La Land, where they navigated through ghosts and goblins at the Fairywood Forever Cemetery, waited on standby behind royal chariots at LAX, flew over the Medieval Tar Pits, and finally found parking on La La Land Boulevard.

Each sight and sound of the city was a treasure for Nickerbacher. Everywhere he looked were other fairy tale creatures. Giants and trolls constructed skyscrapers, hobbits rode skateboards, unicorns pulled carriages for sightseers, elves provided personal training for movie stars, and pixies sold decorated wings to children.

Nickerbacher stepped off the curb and quickly jumped back as a harpy sped by driving a cab. He nearly knocked into Medusa, a meter maid in the process of turning an angry driver into stone. Fortunately, Nickerbacher was saved from further incident when the prince and princess pulled up on Happenstance's horse.

"There are so many different fairy tale creatures!" Nickerbacher said. "And they're walking among humans!"

Then Nickerbacher noticed the iconic La La Land sign and convinced the prince and princess to hike up Royal Canyon for a better view. When they got to the top, the entire city stood before them. The ocean was at a distance and the buildings looked like an architectural model. He started to get sad, then angry that there was not a dragon anywhere. He could only manage to take a half-hearted selfie.

Reporters and photographers swarmed Nickerbacher. "A dragon! A dragon here in La La Land!"

They snapped his photo and shoved microphones in his face. "Tell us why you've come," one said. "Are you going to eat us?"

"Not without a little paprika," Nickerbacher said.

They gave a nervous laugh, but pressed in closer and kept shouting.

Prince Happenstance stepped in front of the crowd. "This dragon is under the supervision of the Prince Guild."

"Under supervision?" a reporter asked. "Does that mean you captured him, Mister..."

"Happenstance," the prince said.

"Fancypants?" the reporter said, scribbling on his notepad.

"Yes. Wait! No!! Prince ***Happenstance***," the prince shouted as his face turned red. "And yes! Under supervision. If you'll excuse me, we have some business to take care of."

Princess Gwendolyn rushed up to them as the reporters moved off. "I found a flyer for a comedy coach."

Nickerbacher took it and read, "ARGYLE O'GRATIN, acting coach, comedy writer, lucky leprechaun." He started to toss it in the trash. "I don't need a coach. I got this."

Gwendolyn plucked it from Nickerbacher's hand. "Let's save it, just in case."

THE LATE KNIGHT SHOW
THE LATE KNIGHT SHOW

Chapter Four
The Audition

After hours of practice and preparation, Nickerbacher flew off to audition for Johnny Kingston As he approached *The Late Knight Show* building, Prince Happenstance dropped off the princess and parked his horse.

Nickerbacher gulped. "Well, this is it."

They stepped into the reception area. There was a pile of ashes sitting at the desk with a nameplate that read "Miss Phoenix".

"Maybe the secretary is on break," Nickerbacher said.

Suddenly there was a flash of fire and a phoenix erupted from the ashes. "Do you have an appointment?" she said.

"Yes," Nickerbacher said. "I went online and...."

"Waste of time. Magical creatures have little chance of getting on the show," Miss Phoenix said. "Dragons? Ha! Never."

"We want to change that," Princess Gwendolyn said. "If Nickerbacher gets on stage, he'll inspire others."

"I don't know," Miss Phoenix said. "I'm already on probation for pooping on the boss's car."

"Miss Phoenix. Do you have children?" Gwendolyn asked.

"Two," she answered. "Why?"

"What do they want to be when they grow up?" the princess said.

"Well, my girl wants to be an astronaut," Miss Phoenix said. "My son wants to be a carrier pigeon for the postal service."

"Don't you want your children to grow up in a world where they're allowed to follow their dreams?" the princess said.

Miss Phoenix considered that. "I'm convinced," she finally said. "Down the hall. Go through the door with the cuckoo clock over the top. Try not to blow it." Then she collapsed back into a pile of ashes.

They strode down the hallway. Nickerbacher was awestruck by the pictures of his idols on the wall: Thaddeus Boondoggle, Scooter McDougall, and Phyllis Pinkerton.

The cuckoo clock sounded as he entered the room.

Nickerbacher jumped up on a makeshift stage and greeted Johnny Kingston. “It’s an honor to meet you, sir.”

“Who let you in here? We don’t allow dragons to audition,” Johnny said.

The prince stepped up. "Excuse me, Mr. Kingston. I'm Prince Happenstance. I put my career on the line with the Prince Guild for this cause. I believe this dragon has potential. If I could change, perhaps you could too?"

"I'm not sure," Johnny said. "People and dragons?" He turned to Nickerbacher and shrugged. "Okay, kid. Let's see what you got."

Nickerbacher took the microphone from the stand and cleared his throat. What was that joke he was going to open with? His mind drew a blank. Johnny tapped a pen on the desk. Nickerbacher cleared his throat again.

"A boy asked me where I got this dragon costume. So I asked him where he got the boy costume. At the toy store?"

Johnny buried his face into his hands. "You got anything better, kid?"

Nickerbacher started to sweat. "Um. How do you like this new floor? During rehearsal, it cracked."

Johnny looked up.

Gwendolyn shook her head, her eyes widened.

Prince Happenstance leaned in.

"It was just a stage I was going through. Seriously, folks, I thought I was going to bring the house down!"

Johnny smiled. "I see something in you, kid. But you're not very funny. Plus, you're a dragon. The Guild will have a fit."

"Nickerbacher will win them over," the princess said. "He can change hearts and minds. Please give him a break."

"What about the novelty of a dragon comedian?" the prince said.

"This *could* be a chance to boost my ratings," Johnny Kingston said.

"I'll promote it throughout the city," Princess Gwendolyn said.

"We'll get you a full house," the prince added.

"All right, kid, but you'd better get a coach. I expect A-list material by the time you get on my stage," Johnny said.

"I promise that he'll work on his act," Gwendolyn said.

"You'll be gobsmacked," Nickerbacher said.

* * *

Nickerbacher and the princess walked out of the building onto La La Land Boulevard. The prince signaled for his horse.

"What happened to all the family material we worked on?" Gwendolyn said.

"I was nervous! I forgot," Nickerbacher said.

"Well, your charm isn't going to get you to the finish line," Gwendolyn said. "We should call that coach. You need polish."

ADVICE
Take it or have it

CHAPTER FIVE
THE COACH

The next day, Nickerbacher met with the new coach. Argyle tipped his tall, green top-hat. "Top o' the mornin' to ye!"

"Howdy," Nickerbacher said. "I'm here to learn about comedy."

"Are ye now?" The leprechaun cracked his knuckles. "Comedy is about the truth, lad, and truth be sometimes sad. But if ye confront all that and more, the audience will then be yours."

Nickerbacher clapped. "Hey, that rhymes!"

"Just talk about real things," Argyle said. "Life can be serious, but sometimes that's what makes the best jokes."

"What about the unjust treatment of dragons?" Nickerbacher asked.

"That's good. Edgy," the coach said. "We can use it."

* * *

Nickerbacher took a break from studying his lines. He did some sightseeing while Gwendolyn and Happenstance passed out flyers in front of the Enchanted Chinese Theatre. He joined tourists on the sidewalk as they watched an Arabian snake charmer, munchkin break-dancers, and The Three Bears on unicycles.

Nickerbacher tried to fit his feet in movie stars' footprints at the entrance of the theatre. Tourists approached him and offered $5.00 to pose for a picture.

On the corner of Fairywood Boulevard and Giantland Avenue, a Sphinx had a street stall called RIDDLE ME THIS.

"Get your riddles! Get your riddles here!" the Sphinx hailed.

"I'll take a riddle," Princess Gwendolyn said.

"What is the creature that walks on four legs in the morning, two legs at noon and three in the evening?" the Sphinx asked.

"A dragon comedian," Princess Gwendolyn said.

"Uh, not even close," the Sphinx said. "What's a dragon comedian?"

Nickerbacher waved.

"It's Nickerbacher." Princess Gwendolyn gestured with her thumb. "He's performing this Friday night. Here are free tickets."

Gwendolyn and Nickerbacher wandered down the boulevard. Prince Happenstance followed on his horse.

"The answer is *man*," the Sphinx called. "Man, you are bad at riddles."

* * *

Nickerbacher was practicing in the mirror in his hotel room when he heard a strange noise outside. He glanced out the window and saw Princess Gwendolyn putting up posters as Papa Dragon followed behind, breathing fire and burning them to a crisp. People were screaming and scattering.

Nickerbacher soared out the window and landed in front of the last poster. As Papa took a breath, Nickerbacher put out his hands. "Papa! Stop!"

"You need to come home," Papa Dragon said. "Now."

"But, Papa! Dragons will *never* have equal rights if I don't perform!" Nickerbacher cried. "I'm *not* a baby."

Papa beat his wings. "Don't be so dramatic!"

"Me!?!" Nickerbacher yelled.

"Mama is worried you'll get hurt." Papa lowered his voice, "So am I."

"I'll be okay, Papa." Nickerbacher folded his arms. "I'm *doing this.*"

"Enough," Papa said. "You're on your own."

He flew off with a roar.

"What if I call your mother?" Gwendolyn said. "I know she'll want to support you."

"Noooo... okay," Nickerbacher said. "Mama is usually on my side. Maybe she'll be able to calm Papa down."

Chapter Six
The Show

Nickerbacher peeked through the curtain. There wasn't an empty seat in the audience, which included all kinds of magical creatures. Griffins and dwarves were scattered throughout the audience. The Sphinx and some friends had a row, and even Santa Claus and his elves were in attendance.

Nickerbacher began pacing. "I don't think I can go on!"

"It's okay, big guy," Princess Gwendolyn said.

Prince Happenstance rushed in with a large bouquet of flowers. "I picked these on the way."

Nickerbacher reached for them. "For me?"

"Um, well, no," the prince said. "They're for... Gwendolyn."

The princess smiled. "You're a goof. But thanks, they're pretty." She plucked the most colorful flower and pinned it on Nickerbacher's lapel.

"I'm so nervous, I'm shaking!" Nickerbacher said.

"Oh, I almost forgot," Gwendolyn said. "A card came for you."

Nickerbacher opened it and a four-leaf clover fell out. "It's from Argyle!" he said. "*Speak ye the truth*. That's what we worked on."

"We believe in you," the princess said. "You've come all this way. Now go and get your dream."

The show began. At long last, Johnny Kingston cued Nickerbacher. "Ladies and gentlemen, what's tall, green, and breathes fire? Besides my mother-in-law, it's the first dragon comedian ever on our program…or anywhere! Give a hand to…Nickerbacher!"

Nickerbacher walked out on wobbly legs. The crowd gasped. The spotlight widened as he greeted the audience. "Thanks for coming, everybody. You know what's funny?"

Nickerbacher suddenly stopped. He squinted and saw Mama and Papa Dragon in the front row.

Papa looked furious. Nickerbacher's heart sank. All his coaching went out the window as his brain froze with fear. Mama gave him a thumbs up.

Nickerbacher took a deep breath. "Um, have you ever tried eating a clock? It's very time consuming."

Johnny Kingston groaned.

Papa Dragon coughed.

Gwendolyn was sitting at the edge of her seat. She held up the four-leaf clover and mouthed, "TELL THE TRUTH!"

"The truth," Nickerbacher said. "The truth is that everyone's so afraid of being different. They hide who they are and try to blend in. But that's crazy! You know what's more unusual than a dragon? An invisible dragon!"

A spattering of giggles scattered through the audience. Papa Dragon turned his head and snorted. Mama Dragon nudged him.

Nickerbacher tilted his head. "So I've decided to stop apologizing for being me. I try to be the best dragon I can.

And when people turn their noses up because of the way I look, I just say, hey, you could fit the whole Prince Guild in there!" He snickered and pointed at Prince Happenstance.

Warm laughter filled the air.

"People who don't like us because we're different are ***afraid*** of the unknown," Nickerbacher said. "Maybe the solution... is to just get to know each other."

Nickerbacher took a few steps forward. "Like, I know how cool I am, and if humans took the time to get to know me, they'd learn that dragons aren't ***all*** angry and serious." Nickerbacher leaped to his toes and raised his arms like a ballerina. "Some tell jokes and do ballet."

He chasséd to the left and signaled the stage manager to lower a piñata.

Nickerbacher twirled and his tail swatted the piñata. "FIRE IN THE HOLE!" he shouted as candy scattered into the audience.

Nickerbacher nodded at two young dragons looking in awe at him. "Boom. You've all been dragooned."

The audience laughed and cheered as Nickerbacher took a bow.

A little grin formed at the edge of Papa's mouth, then *he* busted a belly laugh. Mama Dragon cried and blew kisses.

The entire house clapped and hollered. Princess Gwendolyn and Prince Happenstance were the first to start a standing ovation. They turned to each other, high-fived and hugged.

Johnny Kingston gestured for Nickerbacher to sit on the couch for a chat. "You did it, Nickerbacher. That was fresh, clever material. I see a new era in comedy on the horizon."

"That means everything coming from you, Mr. Kingston," Nickerbacher said.

"Call me Johnny," he said with a wink.

After the show, Mama and Papa came backstage. Nickerbacher flashed a sheepish grin. "You're not mad at me?"

"You got guts, son," Papa Dragon said. "How could I stay mad?"

"He won't say it, but Papa is proud of you!" Mama Dragon said.

Princess Gwendolyn rushed in holding hands with Prince Happenstance. "Nickerbacher! You really *did* bring down the house! Everybody loved you!"

She kissed Nickerbacher on the cheek then turned to the prince. They started to hug, but at the last second, she kissed him, too. His eyes lit up with delight.

The young dragons from the audience tapped Nickerbacher on his shoulder.

"Can we have your autograph?"

Nickerbacher smiled. "Sure!"

"How do you feel about being famous?" one asked.

Nickerbacher thought a moment. "You know what happened to the dragon whose dream came true?"

"What?" they asked.

He glanced over his shoulder at the prince and princess and beamed at Mama and Papa. "He lived happily ever after."

Made in the USA
Middletown, DE
29 December 2016